·THE · WAY · IT · WORKS ·

Heat

NEIL ARDLEY

NEW YORK

First American publication 1992 by New Discovery Books, Macmillan Publishing Company, 866 Third Avenue, New York, NY 10022

Macmillan Publishing Company is part of the Maxwell Communication Group of Companies

First published in 1991 by
Heinemann Children's Reference,
a division of Heinemann Educational Books Ltd,
Halley Court, Jordan Hill, Oxford OX2 8EJ

Library of Congress Cataloging-in-Publication Data
Ardley, Neil
    Heat / Neil Ardley
      p. cm. — (The way it works)
    Summary: Defines heat and discusses its properties, origins, and uses.
    ISBN 0-02-705666-X
    1. Heat — Juvenile literature. [1. Heat] I. Title.
    II. Series
    QC256.A72   1992
    536—dc20   91-29057

Photographic credits
t = top b = bottom r = right l = left

4 ZEFA; 5 Science Photo Library; 7, 8, 9 ZEFA; 14 Michael Blacker; 15 ZEFA; 16 Science Photo Library; 19 ZEFA; 21 Trevor Hill; 25 Robert Bosch Appliances Ltd; 28t Robert Harding Picture Library; 32t Science Photo Library; 35 Trevor Hill; 36 NHPA; 37 Planet Earth Pictures; 41 NHPA; 42 Science Photo Library

Designed and produced by Pardoe Blacker Limited, Lingfield, Surrey, England
Artwork by Terry Burton, Tony Gibbons, Jane Pickering, Sebastian Quigley, Craig Warwick and Brian Watson
Printed in Spain by Mateu Cromo

91 92 93 94 95 10 9 8 7 6 5 4 3 2 1

Note to the reader
In this book there are some words in the text which are printed in **bold** type. This shows that the word is listed in the glossary on page 46. The glossary gives a brief explanation of words which may be new to you.

Contents

What is heat?

Heat is a form of **energy**. We make and use heat energy all the time. Our bodies need heat to keep working.

Many of our machines also make and use heat. When it is cold, heaters keep our houses, schools, and cars warm. Water heaters give us plenty of hot water for washing and bathing. Cars and aircraft make heat by burning **fuel**.

▼ There is great heat inside the earth. The heat can make solid rock melt to a liquid that flows like a river. The heat also turns liquids into gases. Gases and liquid rock from inside the earth may be pushed up to the surface through a crack called a volcano.

It happens with heat

Every action needs energy to make it happen. Sometimes this is heat energy. Cars and aircraft get the energy to move from the heat made by burning fuels. We cook food with heat energy.

Electricity is another form of energy. Electric stoves change electricity into heat energy to cook our food. We can change heat into other forms of energy too. Most of the electricity we use is made from heat. In fact, almost all the world's energy originally comes from heat. The source of all this heat is the sun.

◄ The heat rays from the sun can make the sand and the people on the beach very hot. Sunshades shelter people from the sun's heat rays. Some of the rays pass through clouds, so the sun warms us even when the sky is cloudy.

Heat on the move

Heat travels across space from the sun to reach the earth. The heat travels as invisible **heat rays**. When the sun warms you, heat rays from the sun are striking your body.

Heat moves through many substances, such as air, water, and metals. When heat enters a substance, its **temperature** rises and the substance feels warmer. A lot of heat can make it too hot to touch. Heat can also move out of a substance. Then it gets colder and its temperature falls. Refrigerators take heat from food to keep it fresh.

Metal objects often feel cold. This is because some heat flows out of your fingertips into the metal as you touch it. So your fingertips become colder.

Heat changes things

Substances change when heat enters or leaves. All substances are made up of many tiny parts called **molecules**. The molecules are always moving. When heat enters a substance, its molecules move faster. When heat leaves, the molecules slow down.

Water, ice, and steam

Water is usually a liquid. When water becomes very cold its molecules slow down. The liquid water changes into a solid called ice. Heating the ice makes the molecules start moving faster. So the ice melts back to liquid water. More heat makes the molecules move faster and faster, until the water boils. The water is changing from a liquid into a gas called steam. When they are heated, many substances change from solids to liquids, and then to gases.

► The earth is warm enough for us to live on it because of the sun. The heat rays from the sun travel through space and warm the earth. The sun is a mass of burning gases.

5

Body heat

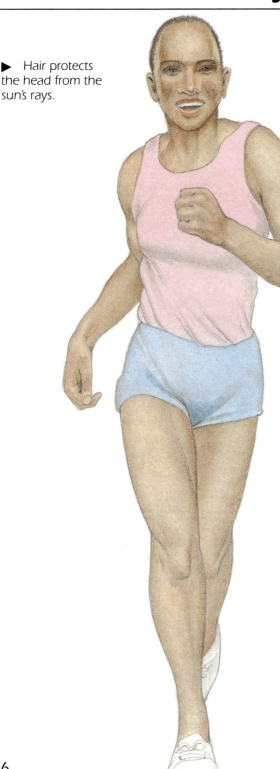

▶ Hair protects the head from the sun's rays.

◀ An athlete speeding around a race track is using and losing heat in several ways. However, the athlete's body is making so much heat that she feels hot at the end of the race.

◀ Skin protects our bodies. Dark pigmentation (skin color) helps to protect the body from the sun's rays. A light-skinned person is more likely to get sunburn. Too much strong sun can damage the skin.

◀ If we get too hot, we sweat. As the sweat evaporates we lose heat and this makes us feel cooler.

Your body is using heat all the time. Heat provides the energy for your body movements. Your chest and lungs move as you breathe. Your heart beats to send blood around your body. Your **muscles** move your arms, legs, and other parts of your body. Without heat energy, you would die.

Some animals, such as snakes, get some of the heat they need from the sun. We get most of the heat we need by eating and drinking. Our bodies break down, or digest, the food and drink to release energy.

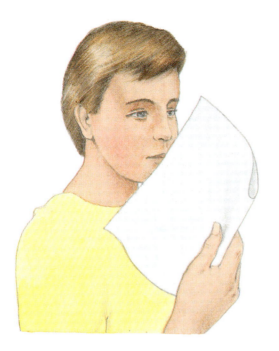

◄ When you fan yourself, you blow air over your skin. The moving air turns more sweat to water vapor and uses up more heat. As heat is lost, the skin becomes cool. This is why the flow of air feels cool.

Heat moves from a warm body into the cool air. In cold weather, we must not lose too much heat to the cold air, so we wear more clothes to keep in our body heat. If we lose too much heat, we shiver with cold. Shivering helps to keep us warm. Movement uses up our energy reserves but also releases heat. Shivering produces a lot of heat to warm the body.

Having a temperature

Your body needs just the right amount of heat to work properly. It needs to stay at about the same temperature all the time. When you are ill, your body temperature may rise or fall slightly. This is why a doctor measures a sick person's temperature with a **thermometer**.

Getting hot and cooling down

When the body gets or makes too much heat, we feel hot. The sun's rays can make us very hot when we are on the beach. Wearing a lot of clothes on a warm day makes us feel hot. This is because the clothes keep in too much of the body's heat. Fast movement, such as running, makes the body produce extra heat.

We can cool down by taking shelter from the sun, or by taking off some clothes to let the body heat escape. **Sweat** comes from holes in the skin called pores. The sweat changes into invisible water **vapor**. Heat energy causes this change. Sweat takes heat energy from the body and cools the body.

▲ When it is very cold, we need to stop our body heat from escaping. Several layers of clothing can be more effective than one thick piece of clothing. It is also important to wear a hat. We lose a tenth of our body heat through the head.

Making fire

People probably first made fire about a million years ago in Africa. Being able to make fire is an important difference between people and other animals.

At first, people used fires to warm themselves and to help keep fierce animals away. Then they found that heating meat in a fire made the meat easier to eat.

About 300 years ago, people started using fire to make energy for machines. Coal, gasoline, wood, and other fuels burn to give heat energy. By burning fuels, people heated water to make steam, which drove the first **steam engines**. Today, **combustion engines** burn gasoline to provide energy for cars and other machines.

Why things burn

When we heat paper and wood, they burst into flames. Other substances, like steel, do not burn however hot they get. Instead, they melt to a liquid.

Burning needs a gas in the air called **oxygen**. The molecules in paper can link up quickly with the molecules of oxygen in the air. This linking produces heat. The linking happens so quickly that the heat builds up and forms a flame. The paper burns to **ashes**.

To link up, the molecules must be moving fast enough to come together. This is why paper must be heated before it will burst into flame. Substances that do not burn have molecules which will not link up quickly with oxygen.

Gasoline and natural gas used in stoves catch fire quickly because they mix easily with air. Paper is thin, has a large surface, and has a lot of air around it. Oxygen molecules from the air and the molecules from the paper are able to come together easily. A lump of wood or coal has a much smaller surface and needs more heat to catch fire.

◀ All fires need oxygen in the air to burn. If we stop air from getting to a fire, it will go out. We use foam, water, and fire blankets to stop air from getting to fires.

▶ Most of the materials in a house will burn if they become too hot. Never put furniture or curtains too close to a lamp, heater, or fire. Put a screen around a fire so sparks cannot jump out. Before going to bed, switch off all heaters and lamps and close doors so that extra air cannot get into rooms.

Wasted heat

When substances burn, they give off smoke and other **fumes**, as well as flames. Coal fires, wood-burning stoves, and gas fires need chimneys to remove the fumes and smoke. A lot of heat from the fire also goes up the chimney. Instead of warming the room, this heat is wasted.

Power stations burn coal or oil to make electricity. Again, the fumes carry heat away up the chimney. About a third of the heat energy is turned into electricity. Only one quarter of the heat made by burning gasoline in a car engine is used to move the car. All fire is wasteful. We still use fire because it gives us **power** and warmth quickly whenever we need it.

Metal from rock

We can get metal from some rocks by heating them. The metal doesn't burn. It melts and becomes liquid. This is called **smelting**. Copper, tin, iron, zinc, and other metals are obtained by this method.

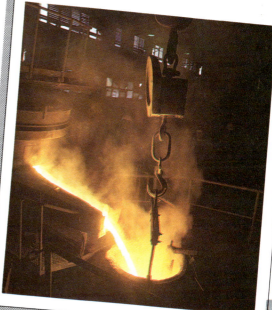

How much heat?

We often need to measure how hot or how cold things are. We measure temperature with a thermometer. It shows the temperature as a number of **degrees**. Nowadays temperature is often measured on the **Celsius** scale. The temperature 20 degrees Celsius is written 20°C.

Water freezes to ice at 0°C. If the temperature gets colder than freezing ice, we use a minus figure. A temperature of -10°C is 10 degrees colder than freezing ice.

Changing size

To measure temperature, a thermometer must change in some way as it gets hotter or colder. Most substances get slightly bigger, or **expand**, when they get hotter. This is because the molecules in the substance move faster and take up more space. When they get colder, most substances get smaller, or **contract**. Common thermometers use the expansion and contraction of liquids to show the temperature.

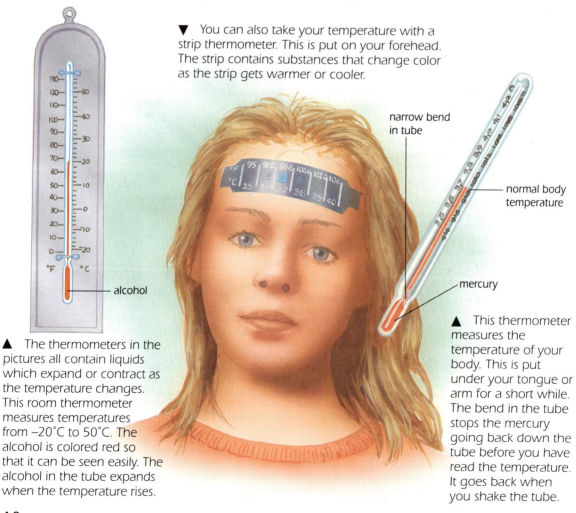

▼ You can also take your temperature with a strip thermometer. This is put on your forehead. The strip contains substances that change color as the strip gets warmer or cooler.

narrow bend in tube

normal body temperature

alcohol

mercury

▲ The thermometers in the pictures all contain liquids which expand or contract as the temperature changes. This room thermometer measures temperatures from −20°C to 50°C. The alcohol is colored red so that it can be seen easily. The alcohol in the tube expands when the temperature rises.

▲ This thermometer measures the temperature of your body. This is put under your tongue or arm for a short while. The bend in the tube stops the mercury going back down the tube before you have read the temperature. It goes back when you shake the tube.

Some thermometers contain liquid mercury, which is a silvery metal. Others contain **alcohol**, which is usually a colorless liquid. The alcohol in thermometers is colored to make the liquid easier to see. If the bulb gets hotter, the liquid expands and rises up the tube. If the bulb gets colder, the liquid contracts and moves down the tube. To read the temperature on a thermometer, look at the number of degrees marked beside the top of the liquid. Our bodies usually have a temperature of about 37°C.

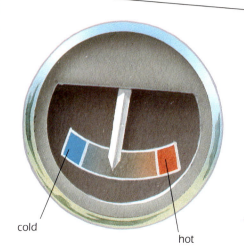

cold

hot

Overheating

If a car engine gets too hot, it may be damaged or cause a fire. The temperature **gauge** in the car does not show degrees. It tells the driver if the engine is too hot or too cold. There is something wrong if the needle enters the red area or falls back to the blue area when the engine is hot.

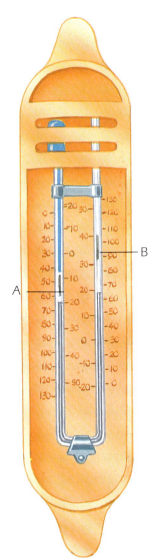

◀ This thermometer is called a Maximum and Minimum thermometer. It can measure the temperature outside. The bulb is filled with alcohol. When it expands it pushes the column of mercury around the tube.

◀ When the temperature falls the mercury rises up the left-hand tube. When the temperature rises, the mercury rises up the right-hand tube.

◀ The bottom of the pin A marks the lowest (minimum) temperature since the thermometer was last read.

◀ The bottom of the pin B marks the highest (maximum) temperature since the thermometer was last read.

Testing the temperature

Thermometers have many uses. If you are ill, the doctor may measure your temperature to help find out what is wrong with you. People who study the weather need to measure the temperature of the air.

In the kitchen, stoves and **freezers** have thermometers. If a stove gets too hot, the food may burn. If the temperature is not hot enough, the food will not be fully cooked. Refrigerators and freezers must stay cold, or the food inside will spoil. Thermometers help us to check that these appliances are working properly. A refrigerator should be at a temperature of between 0°C and 5°C and a freezer should be between -18°C and -25°C.

11

Heat control

Many of the machines in our homes make heat, such as room heaters, irons, and stoves. The machines need to be controlled so that they make the right amount of heat. The heat of an iron presses the wrinkles out of clothes. The iron must be very hot to press cotton clothes, but a very hot iron will make wool burn.

Most heat machines contain a device called a **thermostat**. This controls the machine so that it produces just the right amount of heat.

On and off

The temperature of the iron can be set by turning a dial. Inside the iron, there is a heater controlled by a thermostat. When the iron has heated up to the right temperature,

the thermostat switches the heater off. The iron loses heat to the clothes and air, and the iron's temperature falls. Then the thermostat switches the heater back on. The thermostat keeps turning the iron's heater on and off so that the iron stays at the right temperature.

Pair of metals

Many thermostats contain a **bimetallic strip**. In an electric iron, the strip made of two different metals holds a switch closed so that electricity flows to the heater. The heater changes the electricity into heat energy. As the strip gets hotter, it bends slowly away and the switch opens. This cuts off the electricity. The strip then cools and straightens, until it closes the switch and the electricity flows again.

▶ Many thermostats contain a bimetallic strip. This is a short strip of two different metals fixed together. When the strip gets hotter, one metal expands slightly more than the other. This makes the strip bend.

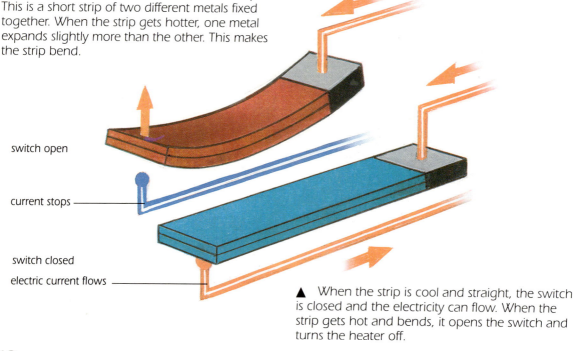

switch open

current stops

switch closed

electric current flows

▲ When the strip is cool and straight, the switch is closed and the electricity can flow. When the strip gets hot and bends, it opens the switch and turns the heater off.

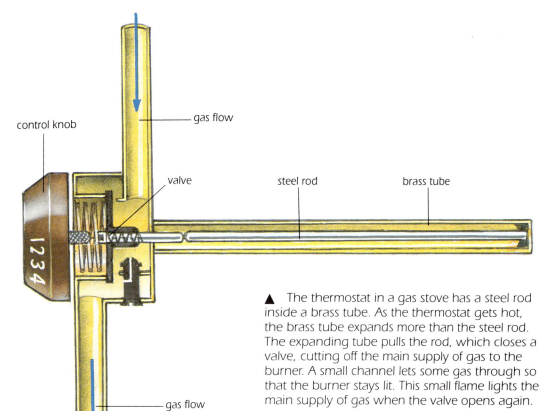

control knob

gas flow

valve

steel rod

brass tube

gas flow

▲ The thermostat in a gas stove has a steel rod inside a brass tube. As the thermostat gets hot, the brass tube expands more than the steel rod. The expanding tube pulls the rod, which closes a valve, cutting off the main supply of gas to the burner. A small channel lets some gas through so that the burner stays lit. This small flame lights the main supply of gas when the valve opens again.

The thermostats of gas heaters and stoves contain a metal tube. When the tube expands, it closes a **valve**. This stops gas flowing to the **burner**.

Control and safety

Thermostats control the temperature of room heaters and water heaters, as well as stoves and irons. Thermostats keep refrigerators and freezers at low temperatures. The thermostat in an electric kettle switches off the electricity when the water in the kettle boils.

Thermostats also help to keep our machines safe. Most machines become warm as they work. Some may get too hot and possibly catch fire. Fire alarms may also contain a thermostat. If a fire starts and makes the room very hot, the thermostat will switch on an alarm bell.

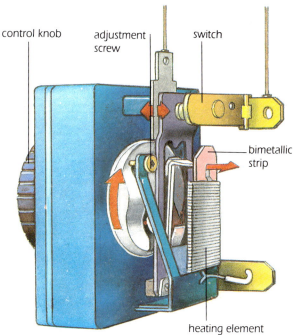

control knob

adjustment screw

switch

bimetallic strip

heating element

▲ This thermostat controls the temperature of a room heater. Turning the knob sets the temperature. Turning the temperature up makes the control cam move the bimetallic strip. It must now bend more before it can open the switch.

Safe heat

Many of the machines in our homes use electricity. The electricity flows through a cable to the house. It travels along wires in the walls and ceilings to lights and **electric outlets**. We can use an electric machine by plugging it in at a wall socket.

Electricity flowing along a wire produces heat. If there is too much heat, electricity may cause a fire. Because of this, we need safety devices to make electricity safe.

Too much electricity

Machines which easily overheat contain thermostats. Other machines, such as radios and televisions, do not usually produce much heat. However, if there is a fault in the machine, too much electricity may flow. Then the machine may become very hot and start a fire.

The wires leading to the machine also become very hot when too much electricity flows. Several machines together take a lot of electricity. This is why you must never plug several machines into one outlet. The extra electricity could heat the wires in the outlet so much that they cause a fire.

Breaking the loop

When an electric machine is working, the electricity flows around a path called a **circuit**. Most of the circuit is a long loop of wire. It goes from the source of electricity through an electrical outlet to the machine and then back to the source. Any gap or break in the circuit stops the electricity flowing. If you unplug or switch off the machine you stop the flow of electricity around the circuit.

Every socket and machine has a safety device. If too much electricity begins to flow, the device breaks the circuit, so the electricity cannot get strong enough to cause a fire.

▶ A fault in the wiring can start a fire that may burn a house down. The electricity in a house must be put in properly and checked. A system of fuses or circuit breakers helps to keep the electricity safe.

◀ One safety device found in houses is called a circuit breaker. This is positioned in the box where the electricity supply enters the home. If a fault in the wiring circuit in the house causes too much current to flow, the circuit breaker automatically cuts off the supply. when the fault is repaired the circuit breaker can be easily reset.

Safety devices

In Great Britain machines use safety devices called **fuses**. A fuse is a thin wire, often inside a tube. This wire melts easily when it becomes too hot.

The fuse forms part of the circuit. When a machine is working normally, electricity flows through its fuse. If a fault causes too much current to flow through the machine, the fuse heats up. The small amount of extra heat melts the wire in the fuse. This breaks the circuit and cuts off the electricity. Once the fault has been repaired, a new fuse is fitted and the electricity will flow again.

In many houses, there are fuses in a box where the electricity supply enters the home. Other houses have safety devices called **circuit breakers**. A switch in the device opens when too much electricity flows and stops the flow. These are particularly popular in the United States.

Slipping and sliding

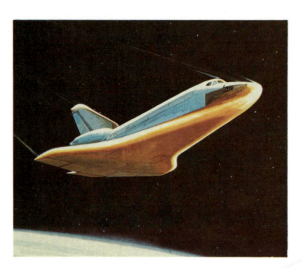

▲ Brakes use friction to turn the energy of a vehicle's movement into heat. Air can act as a brake. Air rubs against a spacecraft returning to earth, and slows the craft down. Friction with the air makes so much heat that the base of the spacecraft glows red-hot.

Do your hands get chilly in cold weather? Rubbing your hands together produces heat and warms them. As you rub, the surfaces of your hands pull against each other. This pull is called **friction**. It slows down the movement of your hands. Friction changes some of the energy you use to move your hands into heat.

Friction happens when any surfaces rub against each other. The amount of friction depends on how rough or smooth the surfaces are. Rubbing the surfaces harder and faster also makes more friction. Friction can produce a lot of heat. For example, if you slide down a rope too fast, the friction between the rope and your hands can make enough heat to burn your hands.

Steering and stopping

We use friction all the time. Without the friction between our shoes and the ground, we could not walk. Instead, we would slide and fall down. The tires on the wheels of a car use friction to grip the road strongly. The car can move forward and steer around corners without skidding and sliding. The friction between the tires and the road produces heat, and the tires get hot.

Car brakes use friction too. When the driver applies the brakes, they rub against the

We slide around on ice and snow for the same reason. As ice skates skim over ice, they produce heat by friction. This heat melts the surface of the ice, forming a thin layer of water under the skates. They slide easily over the water and we are able to move fast. The water may freeze again as soon as we have passed.

▲ Ice is slippery because sliding produces a layer of water on the surface of the ice. Toboggans and skis slide over snow for the same reason.

wheels. Friction makes the wheels slow down and stop. This produces a lot of heat. Stopping a car moving at 60 miles an hour gives enough heat to boil a quart of water!

Sliding over water

When you rub your hands together to wash them, they do not get warm. This is because the soapy water between the surfaces of the hands keeps them apart. The water causes less friction. So the hands slide easily over the water.

Helping machines move

Car engines, bicycles, and many other machines have moving metal parts. There is a lot of friction when metals rub against each other. The metals become very hot and may bend or break. So we cover the moving metal parts of a machine with a thin layer of **oil**. The surfaces of the moving parts slide easily over the oil with little friction. This is called **lubrication**. Without oil, some of the machine's energy is turned into heat by friction. Less energy is needed to keep well-oiled parts moving.

Strike a light

People first made fire using friction. Twirling a stick in a hole in a piece of wood makes enough heat to set fire to small twigs or **tinder**. Striking pieces of hard rock together produces bursts of heat called sparks. A spark can set fire to, or **ignite**, tinder. These were early methods of making fire.

We use similar ways of making fire today. When we light a match, we rub the head of the match hard against a surface. This gives enough heat by friction to ignite the powder in the head. A lighter uses a spark from a flint to ignite a fuel, which is usually gas. A match produces a flame because the powder in the head of the match is made of special **chemicals**. These catch fire and burn rapidly when they are heated.

Bangs and blasts

Chemicals that burn very fast are used in **explosives**. The burning chemicals make the air around the explosive so hot that the air expands very quickly. People nearby can hear and feel expanding air as a blast. The blast and the heat of the explosives in bombs kill people and destroy buildings.

▲ One way of making fire is by rubbing two pieces of wood together. The round stick is held between the palms and twirled in a hole in another piece of wood. Dry moss and twigs have been placed around the hole. After a few minutes, the wood heats up and sets fire to the twigs.

Inside a gun, a tube called a cartridge contains a bullet and fast-burning chemicals called **propellants**. When the gun is fired, the propellants ignite. The burning propellants produce a lot of expanding gas, which pushes the bullet out of the gun. One kind of gun fires a metal case called a shell

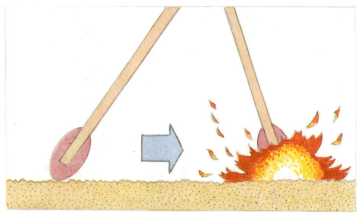

◀ We light a match by striking it. There is a strip of rough sandpaper on the side of the matchbox. When you strike the match along the strip it makes lots of heat by friction. This ignites the chemicals in the head of the match. Safety matches need extra chemicals before they will ignite. The extra chemicals are in the strip. Safety matches will not light if you strike them on any other surface.

using propellants. The shell also contains explosives which may blow up when the shell hits an object.

People may use explosives in other ways. Explosives help people to dig mines and build roads by breaking up hard rocks. Old buildings are sometimes demolished and cleared away using explosives.

Fire in the sky

Fireworks contain chemicals which burn easily, but usually not as quickly as explosives. Some fireworks contain fast-burning chemicals which explode. Rockets have propellants in the bases of their tubes. When we light the paper at the base, the

▲ The chemicals in fireworks burn with brilliant colors or give showers of sparks.

propellants ignite. Expanding gases rush from the propellants and push the rocket upward into the sky.

Even the biggest space rockets are moved by propellants. A **rocket engine** may burn solid propellants like firework rockets. Once they ignite, the rocket engines continue to burn until all the propellant is used up. The engines of space rockets that carry **astronauts** often burn liquid propellants. These engines can be turned on and off many times.

Heating the home

We need heaters to warm the air in our homes when the weather is cold. We also need to heat water for washing. Many homes have **central heating** systems that do both these things.

Heaters need energy to make heat. Most heaters get their energy from electricity or from burning fuels, such as gas, oil, coal, coke, and wood. The energy of the sun's rays is sometimes used for heating too. Once the heat is made, it has to travel to reach us wherever we need it.

▼ A fan heater has a fan which blows air over electric elements. The fan helps the warm air to move around the room.

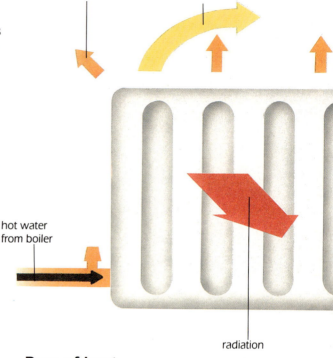

conduction   convection

hot water from boiler

radiation

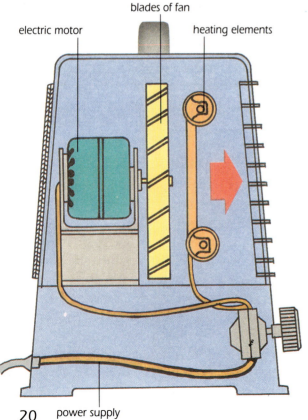

electric motor

blades of fan

heating elements

power supply

Rays of heat

The sun's rays travel millions of miles through space to reach us here on earth. All hot things give out heat rays that travel through the air or space. We call this **radiation**. Radiated heat also comes from coal fires and from electric fires.

Many homes are heated by **radiators**. Hot radiators give out heat rays.

Spreading heat

If you take a hot water bottle to bed, the bottle's warmth spreads into your body. Heat passes through many substances. This movement of heat is called **conduction**.

A hot radiator warms the home by conduction more than by radiation. The heat spreads through the metal sides of the

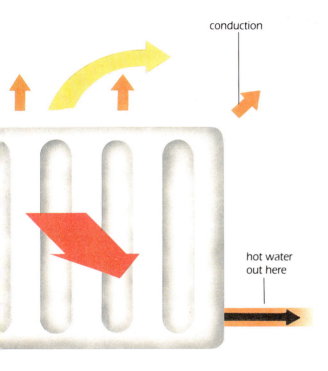

conduction

hot water
out here

▲ A radiator warms a room by radiation, conduction and convection. Heat rays from the hot metal sides warm the room by radiation. The metal sides also heat the surrounding air by conduction. The warm air rises up the room by convection. This radiator get its heat from hot water pumped into it from a boiler.

radiator and warms the air next to it. Conduction also helps to heat the radiator. Many radiators have water from a **boiler** flowing through them. The boiler does not boil the water, but makes it very hot. Heat from a burner or an **electric element** at the bottom of the boiler starts to spread into the water by conduction. Hot water from the boiler may also heat the water that goes to faucets around the house.

Rising heat

When the water in the boiler gets hot, it expands in size. This makes the water lighter, and it rises in a movement called **convection**. More cold water flows into the bottom of the boiler to take its place. This water is heated and rises in turn. The hot water may rise up pipes from the boiler by convection. The water is often forced through pipes by a water pump instead.

Air also carries heat by convection. The hot air around a heater rises. The rising warm air carries heat around the room. Convection heaters warm rooms in this way. The heat from radiators also moves about the home by convection. Any liquid or gas will transfer heat by convection.

Conducting heat

Substances which pass heat easily, such as metals, are good conductors. Glass, wood, and many other substances do not conduct heat easily. These substances are called heat **insulators**. This saucepan is made of metal so the heat transfers quickly to the food. The handle is made of wood so that it does not get too hot to hold.

Heating with wires

Electric heaters are very useful. We can carry small electric heaters around the house and plug them in wherever there is an electrical outlet. The machines give off heat as soon as the electricity is switched on. They do not give off smells or gases, like the heaters that burn fuels.

Some homes have large electric heaters, which store the heat. These **storage heaters** make heat at night. They work at night because electricity is cheaper. Storage heaters release the heat slowly, so they stay hot and warm the room during the day.

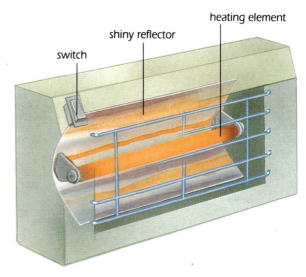

▲ The back of this electric heater has a shiny surface to help send the heat rays from the glowing element out into the room.

▼ This room has heating under the floor. Electricity flows through loops of wire in the concrete. A layer of heat insulator stops heat passing into the ground.

Loops of heat

Every electric heater has a heating element that contains a loop or coil of wire. As the electricity pushes down the wire, it uses energy. The wire acts as a force against, or has **resistance** to, the electricity. The energy changes into heat energy. This makes the wire hot. Long thin wire resists electricity much more than short thick wire. So a long thin wire gives off a lot of heat when electricity flows through it.

The long thin wire in an element is shaped into a loop or coil to save space. For safety, the wire is often surrounded by an electrical insulator. The insulator keeps the electricity in but allows the heat to escape through it.

Heat above and below

Some houses have long loops of wire under the floor and in the ceiling. When electricity flows through them, the loops make the whole floor and ceiling warm. Like storage heaters, the floor and ceiling can be heated at night and will continue to give warmth during the day.

An **electric blanket** also contains loops of wire. The blanket usually goes over the sheets on the bed. Some electric blankets warm the bed and then are switched off before the person gets in. Others are left switched on to keep the bed warm during the night.

Safe heat

Electric blankets can harm us if they become too hot or if electricity escapes from their wires. A thermostat stops the electric blanket becoming too hot. The loops of wire in the blanket are covered with an electric insulator to keep the electricity in.

Electricity flows easily through water. For this reason, electric heaters must never be switched on when they are wet. A wet electric blanket can be very dangerous. It is not safe to use ordinary electric heaters in bathrooms.

▼ The back window of this car has a defroster. There are electric wires in the glass. The driver can switch on the heater when the glass becomes misty and it clears in a few minutes.

Cooking

grill

gas burner

hob

controls

oven

◀ This gas stove has the same features as an electric one. It has a hob, grill and oven. But the heat comes from flames of burning gas instead of electric wires.

Long ago, people found that holding raw meat on a stick over a fire made the meat easier to eat. People learned to use heat to cook in different ways. Sometimes they fixed the food just above the flames. This is called grilling. Sometimes they put the food in pots over the flames. This boils or stews the food. People also discovered that they could cook food slowly in ovens made out of stones or clay. They heated the stones first by lighting a fire inside them or under them. Stones and

clay will store heat for a long time. These sorts of ovens are still used in many countries. The main problem is controlling the amount of heat reaching the food.

We cook in much the same way today. However, instead of burning wood or other solid fuels, we usually use electricity or gas. These can be switched on and off as we want them so we can control the amount of heat much more easily. A thermostat keeps the oven at the right temperature.

24

Cooking with electricity

The cooking part of a stove is called a burner. An electric stove usually has several heating elements in the shape of rings or disks. A strong electric current makes the burner glow red-hot. Food can be boiled, fried, or stewed by placing the food in pots and pans on the burner. Some electric stoves have **ceramic** burners which are smooth like glass. Heating rings inside the burner glow or light up as they get hot.

The oven of the stove is like a large box with electric elements at the sides or at the top and bottom. Material covering the elements cuts down the radiation of heat rays, which could burn the food. The air in the oven gets hot and moves around by convection. When this hot air touches the food, the air transfers heat to the food by conduction. This method heats the food all around and not just from below like on the burner. Some ovens have fans to blow the heated air around the food. This helps the heat to reach the food more quickly and to cook the food more evenly. Many ovens have glass inner doors so that the cook can see the food without letting the hot air out of the oven or cold air in.

Most stoves also have grills, which contain uncovered elements. Heat rays from the red-hot element brown the food placed under the grill. It can also be used to keep food and plates warm.

◀ The rings on this ceramic burner light up as they cook. In them are powerful electric lights called halogen bulbs which produce heat rays as well as light.

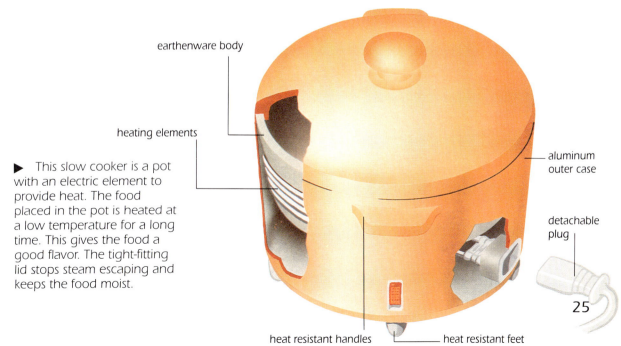

earthenware body

heating elements

▶ This slow cooker is a pot with an electric element to provide heat. The food placed in the pot is heated at a low temperature for a long time. This gives the food a good flavor. The tight-fitting lid stops steam escaping and keeps the food moist.

aluminum outer case

detachable plug

heat resistant handles

heat resistant feet

25

Burning bread

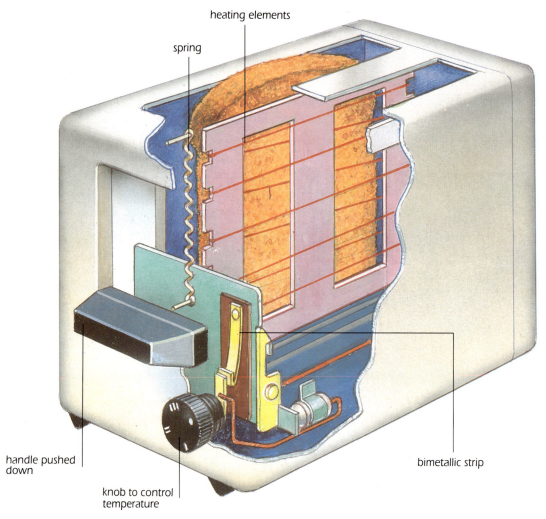

spring

heating elements

handle pushed
down

knob to control
temperature

bimetallic strip

We can cook some things without stoves. Toast is very easy to make. We just need to heat a slice of bread until it begins to turn brown. When the heat has started to burn the surface of the bread, the toast is ready. If the bread is heated too long, it will begin to get black and may even catch fire.

In the past, people made toast by holding bread in front of a fire. Today we make toast by putting bread either under the grill of a stove or in an electric toaster.

▲ Electric toasters have timers. You set the timer to cook the toast just the right shade of brown. Wholewheat bread usually takes a little longer to toast than white bread. Some toasters can take slices of different thicknesses.

Inside a toaster

There are heating elements on either side of the slots in an electric toaster. You put the slices of bread in the slots.

The slices of bread stand on a rack connected to a spring in the toaster. Pushing the handle lowers the rack and stretches the spring. When the rack reaches the bottom of the toaster, a catch holds the rack down. The heating elements switch on.

There is a bimetallic strip beside the catch. The toaster heats the strip as well as the bread. As the strip gets hot, it bends and pushes the catch to release the rack. This happens after the set time. When you increase the toasting time, the strip has to bend more and takes a longer time to release the catch.

Once the catch is released, the heating elements switch off. The spring pulls the rack back up, and the toast pops out of the slots on top of the toaster.

Tasty sandwiches

Sandwiches can be made into very tasty hot snacks by toasting them in an electric sandwich toaster. The slices of bread are buttered on the outside. The filling is put between the unbuttered sides. The sandwiches are placed between two metal plates which contain heating elements. When the toaster is switched on, the plates become hot and cook the sandwich. The hot butter stops the bread from sticking to the plates. It also makes the outside of the sandwich crisp and brown.

heating elements

▶ You can make toasted sandwiches with lots of different fillings. The heavy plates of the toaster push the edges of the sandwich together and seal them. The sealed edges help to stop runny fillings, like melted cheese, from oozing out of the sandwich.

Saving heat

◀ In many parts of the world, people use ovens made of thick mud or bricks. Some ovens, like this baker's oven, are set into the wall. This helps to stop heat escaping and so less fuel is needed.

When we use heat we use fuels such as wood, coal, gas, or electricity. Electricity is also made by burning fuels, such as coal and oil. Most of these fuels took millions of years to form. We must use the fuels carefully so that our supplies last for a long time. We need to save heat whenever we can. Saving energy is called **energy conservation**.

Conservation in cooking

There are several ways we can save heat while cooking. The sides of an oven contain layers of a good heat insulator. This stops much heat escaping from the oven.

A well-shaped pan also helps to save heat. A good pan has a broad, flat base which fits over the whole gas or electric burner. Then all the heat passes into the base and does not escape up the sides of the pan. Some pans have a base of copper, which conducts heat well. In this way the heat passes quickly through the base to the food.

▼ The Chinese often cook food using steam. Different kinds of food are placed one above the other in containers. All the food can be cooked in one pan. The containers are made of bamboo, which is a good heat insulator. It helps to keep the food warm after it is cooked.

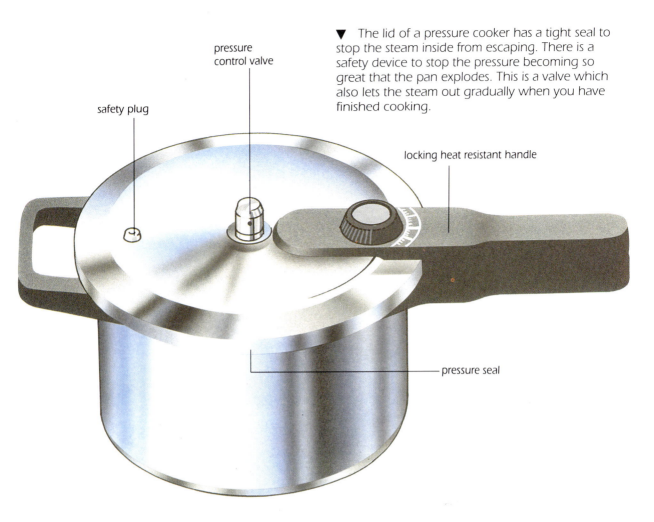

pressure
control valve

safety plug

▼ The lid of a pressure cooker has a tight seal to stop the steam inside from escaping. There is a safety device to stop the pressure becoming so great that the pan explodes. This is a valve which also lets the steam out gradually when you have finished cooking.

locking heat resistant handle

pressure seal

Speed with steam

Another way of saving heat is to cook food very quickly in a special pan. The pan cooks food using hot steam under great **pressure**. So the pan is called a **pressure cooker**.

When water is heated in an ordinary pan, the water boils to steam. The steam presses the lid of the pan up and escapes. The lid of a pressure cooker fits very tightly. When water boils to steam in a pressure cooker, the steam cannot escape. As the steam is heated, the pressure and temperature of the steam increase. The steam becomes much hotter than the steam in an ordinary pan or kettle. Food cooks quickly in such hot steam.

Using a pressure cooker

A little water is put into the pressure cooker. The food is placed in containers that fit inside the cooker. The lid is put on to seal the cooker, which is heated on the stove. The water inside the cooker boils quickly. The steam, which cannot escape, surrounds the food.

The food cooks faster as the steam becomes hotter. The temperature of the steam is controlled by a valve on the lid of the pressure cooker. If the steam becomes too hot, the valve opens and lets some steam escape. This lowers the pressure and temperature of the steam.

Cooking with rays

We usually use heat rays to cook food. However, another kind of ray called a **microwave** can also cook food. A **microwave oven** uses up much less fuel than an ordinary oven. The oven works by electricity but uses very little power and cooks food much more quickly than an electric or gas stove or even a pressure cooker. The heat rays in an ordinary stove cannot pass quickly through food. At first, only the surface of the food becomes hot. The heat slowly spreads through the food by conduction and starts cooking the middle. Microwave radiation can pass quickly through food. So a microwave oven cooks food at the surface and in the middle at the same time.

▼ When you use a microwave oven, you set the temperature and time for the food to cook on the control panel. A bell sounds when the food is ready. Some foods only take a few minutes to cook.

The rotating reflector blades send the microwaves to all parts of the oven.

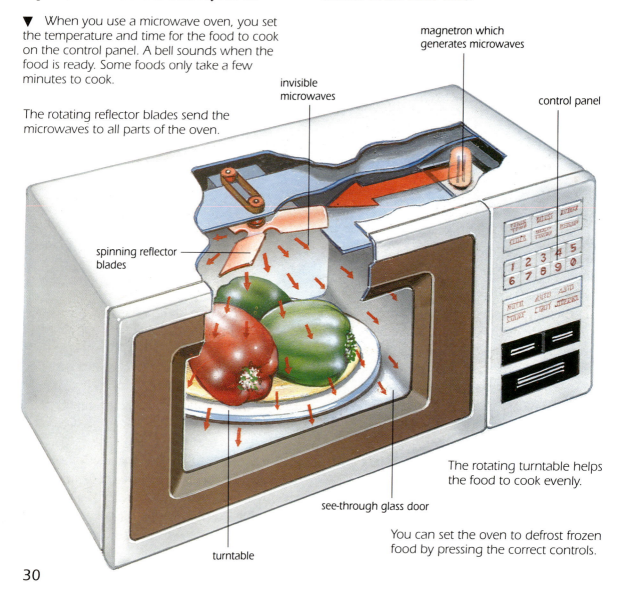

magnetron which generates microwaves

invisible microwaves

control panel

spinning reflector blades

The rotating turntable helps the food to cook evenly.

see-through glass door

turntable

You can set the oven to defrost frozen food by pressing the correct controls.

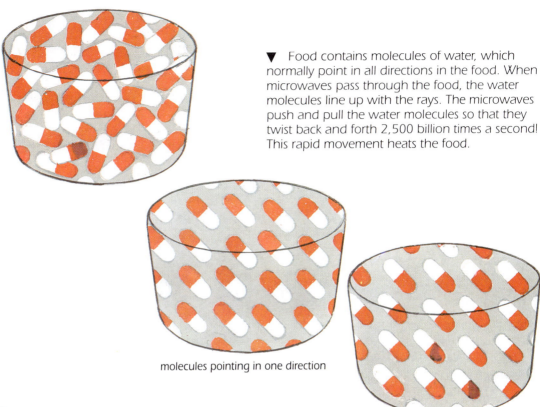

molecules before and after microwaving

▼ Food contains molecules of water, which normally point in all directions in the food. When microwaves pass through the food, the water molecules line up with the rays. The microwaves push and pull the water molecules so that they twist back and forth 2,500 billion times a second! This rapid movement heats the food.

molecules pointing in one direction

molecules pointing in the opposite direction

Making waves

When a microwave oven is switched on, a device called a **magnetron** produces the microwaves. The rays hit spinning metal blades at the top of the oven. Microwaves cannot pass through metal. Instead, the blades **reflect** the microwaves through the oven. The microwaves also reflect off the metal sides of the oven and enter the food from all directions.

In an ordinary oven, the surface of the food becomes very hot and may turn brown. Microwaves cook all through the food at the same time and so the surface does not brown. Some microwave ovens contain heating elements to brown the food after it is cooked. A microwave oven may also have a turntable which moves the food around to heat it evenly.

Using a microwave oven

A microwave oven is easy to use as well as quick. The cook places the food in pottery, glass, or paper containers. Microwaves cannot travel through metal but will pass through pottery and paper.

The container has no liquid molecules. So the microwaves do not make the container hot. The cook can lift the container out of the oven with bare hands. The food can even be put on a plate before it is cooked. When the food is ready, it can be served right away on the plate. Although the food is hot, the plate is only warm.

Keeping heat in

When the weather is cold we put on more clothes to stay warm. The layers of cloth stop much of the heat escaping from our bodies. They do this because they trap layers of air. Moving air can carry away heat by convection, but trapped air lets very little heat pass through it. It acts as an insulator.

We can save heat energy by insulating our homes to keep the heat in. In cold weather we burn a lot of expensive fuel to warm our homes. The heat can escape through the roof, walls, and windows.

A hat for a house

The heaters in a home warm the air. The warm air rises and carries heat upward.

To keep the heat in people can lay thick felt or a **fiberglass** mat on the floor of the loft or attic under the roof. Both felt and fiberglass have tangled fibers which trap air. The trapped air prevents heat from passing through into the roof. The felt and fiberglass keep the house warm just as a woolly hat keeps your head warm.

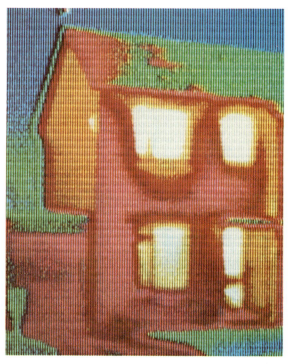

▲ This photograph was taken with special film that picks up heat rays. It shows the heat escaping from a typical house. The color coding ranges from white to orange for the warmest areas through green and blue for the coolest. Heat loss is shown by the red areas.

► This house has been built to keep in as much heat as possible. The round domes and walls are covered with white plastic which stops almost all heat escaping from the house. Houses like this need very little heating to keep warm.

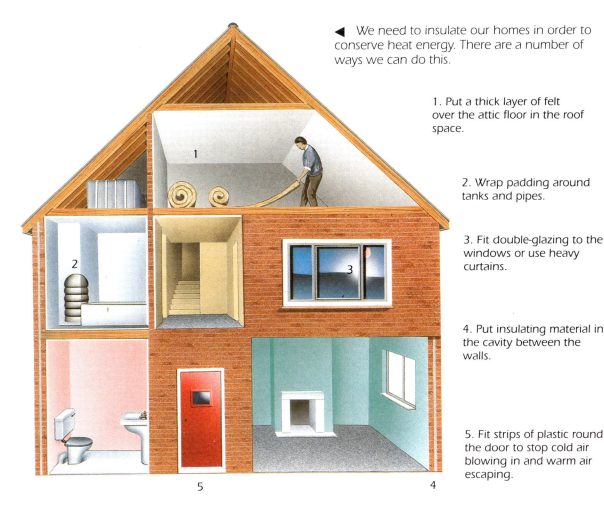

◄ We need to insulate our homes in order to conserve heat energy. There are a number of ways we can do this.

1. Put a thick layer of felt over the attic floor in the roof space.

2. Wrap padding around tanks and pipes.

3. Fit double-glazing to the windows or use heavy curtains.

4. Put insulating material in the cavity between the walls.

5. Fit strips of plastic round the door to stop cold air blowing in and warm air escaping.

Hollow walls

Heat can also escape through the walls of a house, even though they are solid and thick. Many houses have **cavity walls**. This kind of wall is really two walls with a narrow gap or cavity between them. Heat cannot pass as easily through the air in the cavity as through solid brick.

Only half as much heat escapes through a cavity wall as through a brick wall. The heat loss can be reduced to a quarter by filling the cavity with **plastic foam**. The foam is made up of lots of tiny holes that trap air. Very little heat can pass through the foam. Other walls have a layer of fiberglass in the middle to keep heat in.

Light in, heat out

Long ago, houses were much darker than they are today. Glass was difficult to make and people could only have small windows. About 200 years ago, people found easier ways of making glass and large windows became common. The large windows let in lots of light, but they also let out lots of heat. A glass pane lets out about twice as much heat as a solid brick wall.

Double glazing works in a similar way to a cavity wall. A double-glazed window is two panes of glass with a layer of air trapped between. The air cuts down heat loss by half. Double glazing also helps to stop loud noises entering from outside.

Keeping drinks hot

Sometimes we need to keep drinks hot for several hours. We can put them in a special container called a **thermos** bottle. The heat in the liquid cannot pass easily through the walls of the container, so the drink stays hot for a long time.

An empty gap

The hot drink is poured into a container made of glass or steel inside the thermos. Like a cavity wall, this container has two walls with a gap between them. However, there is no air trapped in the gap. Instead, all the air has been pumped out from the gap to leave a **vacuum**. This is why the flask is sometimes called a vacuum or thermos bottle.

▲ Wide-necked vacuum jars can be used to store food that is not liquid, such as ice cream. These people put their thermos bottles inside a cool box to make sure the ice cream stays frozen.

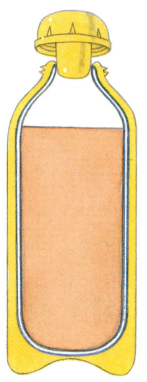

◄ A thermos bottle keeps drinks hot or cold for several hours.

◄ The screw cap and stopper prevent heat loss because they fit tightly. However, this is still the weak point of the container and heat escapes very slowly.

◄ The glass container has two walls. The air is pumped out of the gap between the walls to make a vacuum.

◄ The silvery surface reflects heat back into the flask.

Heat travels by conduction, convection and radiation. A thermos bottle prevents heat moving in all of these ways. Heat can spread through many substances by conduction, but it cannot spread through a vacuum. The empty gap has no air to carry heat away by convection. Heat rays can cross a vacuum by radiation, so the inner and outer surfaces of the vacuum container are made shiny, like a mirror. The shiny surfaces reflect the heat rays back into the hot drink.

Coolers

Boxes called coolers can keep picnic food and drinks cool for a few hours. The sides of the cooler are filled with materials which are good heat insulators. They help to keep the heat out. If you put ice in the box, this takes up any heat which gets in. The food and drinks inside the cooler stay cool.

▼ Hospitals need parts of a body to be brought from one place to another for transplant operations. The organs such as kidneys have to be kept at the right temperature. They are taken in special vacuum containers.

Hot or cold

A thermos bottle can also keep cold drinks and ice cream cold. This is because such a container is just as good at keeping heat out as keeping heat in. Heat from outside cannot pass through the walls of the container to warm up the cold drink or ice cream.

The outside cover of a thermos bottle is often made of plastic, which helps keep the heat in or out. The stopper in the top is also made of a heat insulator such as cork or plastic. However, a thermos bottle does not keep food and drinks hot or cold forever. Heat passes slowly into or out of it, mainly through the stopper.

High and harsh

◀ These people are wearing light-colored clothes to keep cool. White materials reflect heat rays. It is also cooler to wear clothes which cover the body.

Many people live in harsh places on the earth. Some people dwell in hot deserts, while others live in the icy Arctic. Sometimes there are even a few people high above the earth, out in space. There it can get hotter that anywhere on earth.

For us to be healthy, our body temperature must stay at about 98°F (37°C). People in harsh places can easily become too hot or too cold. Such people wear special clothes to help the body stay at the right temperature.

Wearing the right clothes

In hot countries, people often wear white clothes. White materials reflect more heat rays than dark materials. White clothes help to keep the heat out.

People who live in cold areas need to keep in their body heat. These people often wear clothes lined with fur or wool. The loose fibers of fur and wool trap air, which prevents heat from escaping. The clothes cover the whole body with no gaps, so cold air cannot get in and chill the body.

Suited for space

Around the earth, there are layers of gases called the atmosphere. It keeps out some of the sun's heat rays during the day. At night, the atmosphere keeps in some of the heat rays. So the atmosphere helps to stop us from becoming too hot or too cold. Out in space, there is no atmosphere to protect us.

Astronauts sometimes leave their spacecraft and work in space. They can survive in space because they wear bulky white spacesuits. Each spacesuit is like a tiny spacecraft.

▼ In Alaska, people wear clothes made from fur or wool to insulate them against the cold.

Layers upon layers

The sun's light is so bright that it could hurt the astronaut's eyes. The helmet of the spacesuit has a dark **visor** to cut out some of the light. The sun's heat rays are also very strong. The shiny spacesuit reflects some of these rays. The outer part of the spacesuit has several layers of insulating materials with air trapped between them. The layers and air help to keep the sun's heat out and keep the body's heat in.

Next to the astronaut's skin is an undergarment lined with narrow tubes. Cold water from a backpack flows through the tubes. The water takes away extra heat so the astronaut does not get too hot.

▶ This spacesuit has 14 very thin layers of fabric to protect the astronaut from the sun's rays.

Rubberized nylon liner A
Five layers of heat-reflecting plastic film B
Four layers of Dacron cotton C
Two layers of fire-resistant plastic D
Two layers of fire-resistant cloth E

A B B B B B C C C D D E E

Freezing but fresh

We can enjoy ice cream and cool drinks in the heat of summer because **refrigerators** keep things cold. Cold food also stays fresh for much longer.

Germs can make food, such as meat, fruit, vegetables, and milk, go bad quickly. Germs cannot grow well at temperatures below freezing. The cold temperature in a refrigerator helps to stop germs from growing and keeps food fresh.

Freezers make food so cold that it keeps for a very long time. In the Soviet Union, **mammoths** that died thousands of years ago were found frozen in ice. The ice had kept the mammoths so fresh that people could eat mammoth steaks!

▼ Raising a wet finger shows which way the wind is blowing. One side of the finger will feel cold. The wind blows from this direction. Where the wind blows on the finger, the water evaporates, making this side of the finger cold.

Blowing cold

If you wet a finger and blow on it, your finger will feel cold. The moving air makes the liquid water on your finger change to invisible water vapor. Like sweat, water needs energy to change to a vapor. The water takes heat energy from your finger. This is why your finger feels cold.

Many liquids can be made to change to a vapor. The change is called **evaporation**. A refrigerator makes things cold by evaporation. The refrigerator was invented in Australia in 1851.

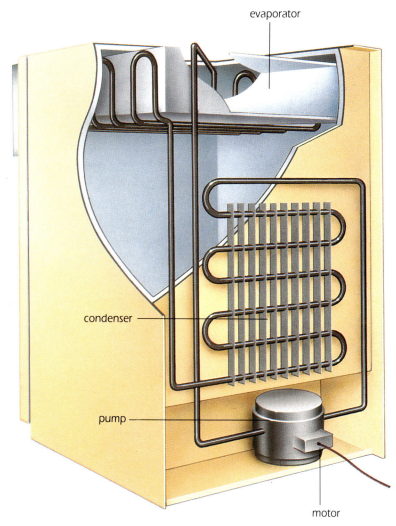

evaporator

condenser

pump

motor

◄ The tube containing refrigerant takes heat away from the refrigerator/freezer and releases it into the air. This is why the sides and back of a freezer or refrigerator feel warm, even though the inside is cold.

In the evaporator, the liquid evaporates and gets very cold. The cold liquid takes the heat out of the refrigerator.

The pump pumps the refrigerant from the evaporator into the condenser.

The refrigerant condenses back to liquid in the condenser. As this happens it gives out the heat taken from the inside.

The motor pumps the refrigerant around the tube.

Inside a refrigerator

Inside the freezer compartment and at the back of the refrigerator is a long tube. It contains a liquid called a **refrigerant**, which evaporates easily. An electric pump pushes the liquid around the tube and back to the pump.

The tube gets wider as it enters the freezer compartment at the top of the refrigerator. The widening lowers the pressure in the tube. This makes the liquid evaporate inside the tube, and the tube becomes very cold. Heat flows into the cold tube from the freezer and refrigerator, making it cold.

The cold vapor in the tube moves around to the pump. The pump squeezes or condenses the gas in the tube, which raises the pressure. This changes the vapor back to a liquid. This change releases the heat energy and makes the liquid warm. The liquid then moves through the tube at the back of the refrigerator. The liquid's heat passes through the sides of the tube into the outside air. In this way, the tube moves heat from the inside of the refrigerator to the outside. The inside of the refrigerator stays cold and keeps food cold and fresh.

Grown under glass

Plants do not grow well in the cold. They need energy to grow. The light and heat from the sun provide much of the energy plants need.

Some plants which we grow for food need more heat than others. Apples and wheat will grow in cool areas, but grapes and tomatoes need warmth to grow well. However, people in cool areas can grow crops which like warmth under glass in **greenhouses**.

More than shelter

We can grow plants from all over the world in greenhouses. Even plants from the **tropics** will grow in cool countries, if the plants are inside a greenhouse. A greenhouse can also make flowers bloom early in the year and helps very young plants to grow.

The glass walls and roof of a greenhouse shelter the plants from cold winds, rain, and snow. The glass panes let in lots of light, which helps the plants to grow.

Heat rays from the sun also pass through the glass panes. The heat rays warm the plants and other things inside. Then they give off their own heat rays. These are different from the sun's rays because they cannot pass through the glass. So the rays are trapped inside the greenhouse. This makes the inside of the greenhouse warmer than the air outside. Some greenhouses also have heaters to help keep the plants warm on very cold days.

◄ Some people have small greenhouses in their yards. They can grow young plants in the greenhouse before planting them out in the garden. This gives the plants a good start.

The sun's rays pass through the glass windows and heat the greenhouse. The heat cannot escape easily so the greenhouse stays warmer than the outside.

Windows help to keep the greenhouse cool in hot weather and let fresh air reach the growing plants.

A thermostat controls a fan to keep the greenhouse at the right temperature.

Pipes or heaters provide extra heat in winter.

A great greenhouse

The earth is a greenhouse too. A lot of the sun's heat rays pass through the atmosphere and warm the surface of the land and sea. The warm surface gives off heat rays that return toward space.

The atmosphere holds in some of the heat rays from the land and sea. This is called the greenhouse effect. The atmosphere keeps us warm, just as the glass in a greenhouse traps heat rays to warm plants. Clouds also help to keep heat in. This is why it can get very cold on a clear night, when there are no clouds.

▲ These plants usually grow in the tropics. They are growing in a greenhouse in Edinburgh, Scotland. The warm atmosphere in the greenhouse is like a tropical climate.

Many people believe that gases from many of the products we make and burning fuels are changing the atmosphere. In the future, the atmosphere may trap more heat, and make the earth warmer. If the earth becomes much warmer, the ice at the poles could melt and the water in the oceans would expand, raising the sea level and flooding part of the land.

41

Power from the sun

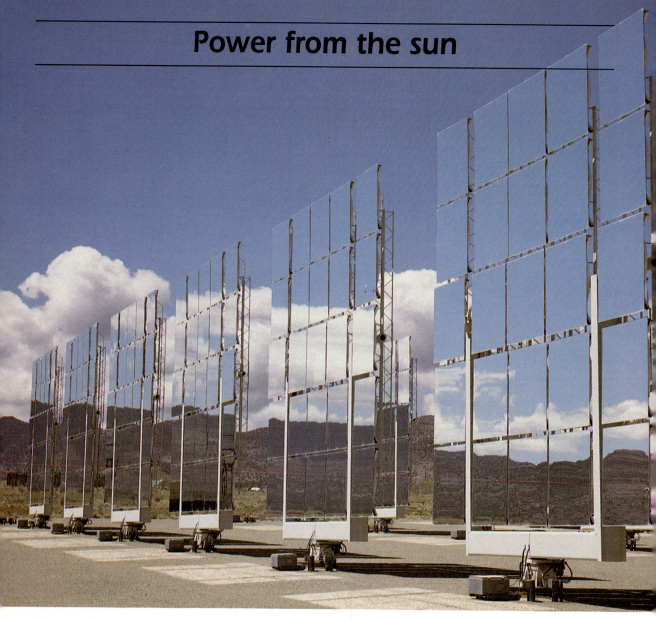

Almost all our energy comes from the sun. Without light and heat from the sun, there would be no animals and plants on earth. Coal and oil are the remains of plants and animals that lived millions of years ago. These fuels stored the energy that came from the sun. When we burn coal and oil, we release this energy.

Electricity is made from the energy of burning fuels. Electricity can also be made

▲ This solar power station is at Albuquerque, New Mexico, a hot and sunny region. Computers control the position of the mirrors so that they always face the sun. The station makes enough electricity to light about 5,000 homes.

using the water in rivers and lakes. This water falls as rain, which comes from water vapor in the air. The sun's heat causes the water vapor to form. So even this electricity really comes from the heat of the sun.

Heat from the sun

We can use the sun's heat directly. Some homes have **solar panels** on the roof. Rays from the sun heat the panels. The panels have thin tubes of water running through them. The water heats up and provides warm water for the home.

People with solar panels do not need to pay for electricity or fuel to heat their water. The heat from the sun is free. However, building and repairing the panels costs money. Solar panels work best in sunny areas. Clouds cut out some of the sun's rays. The panels still work in cloudy areas, but do not give as much heat.

Some houses also have large glass windows that take in the sun's heat. The windows warm the air inside like the panes of glass in a greenhouse.

Electricity from the sun

We can get electricity from sunlight. Some small machines, like calculators, have **solar cells** that turn light into weak electricity. **Solar power stations** turn the sun's heat rays into the strong electricity used in homes.

Solar power stations are built in places such as deserts, where it is sunny most of the time. The power station has a high tower surrounded by a thousand or more mirrors on the ground. The mirrors are placed so that they reflect the sun's heat rays onto a **furnace** in the tower. The rays from all the mirrors meet at the furnace, which gets very hot. Heat from the furnace boils water to make steam. The hot steam drives an electricity **generator.**

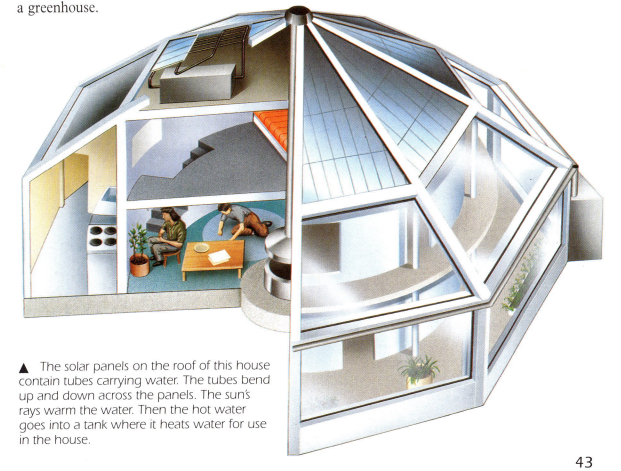

▲ The solar panels on the roof of this house contain tubes carrying water. The tubes bend up and down across the panels. The sun's rays warm the water. Then the hot water goes into a tank where it heats water for use in the house.

Did you know?

Heating the earth

To produce as much heat as the earth gets from the sun, we would have to put a one-bar electric heater on every square foot of the earth's land and sea.

Hot and hasty

The supersonic airplane Concorde flies so fast that friction with the air makes the outside of the aircraft get hotter than boiling water.

Super heat

The temperature at the center of the sun is about 29 million°F. Scientists have produced temperatures of about 360 million°F in machines called fusion reactors.

Sudden fire

Haystacks can suddenly catch fire on their own. Damp hay inside the stack rots and makes heat. The heat may become great enough to set the dry part of the stack on fire.

Hottest place in the world

The highest temperature ever recorded at the surface of the earth is 136°F (58°C) in Libya. At the center of the earth, the temperature is about 8132°F (4500°C). Some power stations use hot water that comes from underground.

Ice breaker

During cold weather, the water inside a pipe may freeze. The expanding ice can crack the pipe. When the ice melts, the water will leak through the cracks in the pipe.

Coldest place in the world

The coldest temperature ever recorded at the surface of the earth is -190°F (-89°C) in Antarctica. The lowest possible temperature is -459.67°F (-273.15°C). It is called absolute zero. Nothing can be cooled below this temperature.

Hot springs

In parts of Iceland, New Zealand and Italy, hot water comes up from under the ground. This hot water can be used to heat homes.

Heat and the future

We burn fuels such as coal, oil, gas, and wood to make heat. We get coal, oil and gas from beneath the land and sea. Supplies of these fuels may run out in the future. We must look for new ways of producing heat.

We may get more heat from plants. We could grow more trees for wood. We can also use plants to make gas and liquid fuels, such as alcohol.

Our best source of heat is the sun, which will last for billions of years. People are trying to find better ways of using the sun's heat for the future.

Glossary

alcohol: a colorless liquid which is made in factories. Alcohol is used in thermometers and as a fuel.

ashes: the powder that is left when something burns.

astronaut: a person who flies in a spacecraft.

bimetallic strip: a strip made of two metals fixed together that bend when the strip gets hot. The two metals are often brass and iron.

boiler: a tank and heater used to provide hot water.

burner: the part of a gas stove or other machine where gas is burned to provide heat.

cavity wall: a wall with a gap in the middle to prevent heat escaping.

Celsius: one of several scales for measuring temperature. On this scale freezing water has a temperature of 0°C, and boiling water has a temperature of 100°C. The sun's surface temperature is 6,000°C.

central heating: a heating system in a house that heats all the rooms and often also provides hot water.

ceramic: made of clay or a similar material. Ceramic objects are not damaged by strong heat.

chemical: any substance that can change when joined or mixed with another substance.

circuit: a complete loop or circle. The path around which electricity flows from the power source to the machine and back again.

circuit breaker: a device which opens a switch to break the circuit when too much electricity flows.

combustion engine: an engine that burns gasoline as a fuel. Most cars have gasoline engines.

conduction: heat moving by spreading through substances such as metals. Not all substances conduct heat well.

contract: get smaller. Most things get smaller when they get colder.

convection: the movement of heat by a liquid or gas. The gas or liquid rises and carries the heat upward.

degrees: the units we use to measure temperature.

double glazing: a window which has an outer and inner pane of glass, with a gap between them.

electric blanket: a special blanket containing loops of wire. When electricity flows, the wires become hot and warm the blanket.

electric element: a device that gives off heat when electricity flows through.

electricity: the form of energy that comes when tiny particles called electrons are made to move. Electricity can travel along wires and be used to make heat in electric heaters.

electric outlet: the socket on a wall where we can plug in electric machines. The electrical outlet supplies electricity from the power station.

energy: the power to do work, and to make things happen. Heat is a form of energy. Other forms of energy include light and electricity.

energy conservation: making and using energy carefully so that the energy is not wasted.

evaporation: changing a liquid into a vapor without boiling the liquid.

expand: get bigger. Most substances get bigger when they get hotter.

explosive: a fast-burning substance that makes a loud blast and a lot of heat when ignited.

fiberglass: a material made of thin threads of glass stuck or tangled together.

freezer: a kind of refrigerator, or a compartment in a refrigerator, which keeps food very cold. Food in a freezer stays fresh for a long time.

friction: a force produced when two surfaces rub together. Friction causes heat.

fuel: a substance that is burned to make energy. Gasoline and coal are fuels.

fumes: the gases formed when something burns. Some of these gases are dangerous.

furnace: an oven used for making large amounts of heat.

fuse: a safety device that controls the flow of electricity.

gas: a substance that will move to fill any space. Air is made up of gases. Air fills all the space around us.

gauge: any device used for measuring something. A thermometer is a temperature gauge.

generator: a machine that changes movement into electricity. The heat energy in steam is often used to produce movement for a generator.

germs: tiny living things that make food go bad. Germs can make us ill.

greenhouse: a building used for growing plants. The walls and roof of the greenhouse are made of glass.

heat rays: a form of heat given off by hot objects including the sun. Heat rays can move through space, air, water, and glass.

ignite: set on fire or catch fire.

insulator: a material which does not let heat or electricity flow through it easily. Plastics and woods are insulators; so is the air.

liquid: a substance that is not a solid or a gas. Liquids flow, like water.

lubrication: placing a liquid, such as oil, between two surfaces so that they slide easily over each other.

magnetron: the part of a microwave oven that produces the microwaves which heat the food

mammoth: an elephantlike animal, which lived thousands of years ago.

microwave oven: an oven that uses microwaves to heat or cook food.

microwaves: invisible rays similar to heat rays.

molecules: the tiny parts of which all things are made. Heat energy makes molecules move faster.

muscles: the parts of the body which help to make movement. Muscles are made of bunches of fibers and are found all over the body.

oil: a slippery liquid, which helps to prevent friction in machines.

oxygen: a gas found in air and water. All animals and plants need oxygen. Without oxygen nothing will burn.

plastic foam: a form of plastic that is light and spongelike, containing many small holes.

power: the supply of energy needed to do something.

power station: a place where the energy from heat or movement is changed into electrical energy which is sent to homes and factories.

pressure: the force with which a liquid or gas presses on the sides of its container, or on anything in the liquid or gas.

pressure cooker: a pan that cooks food quickly by using very hot steam at high pressure.

propellant: a material that burns in a cartridge to fire a bullet, or the fuel used in a rocket.

radiation: the movement of heat in the form of heat rays.

radiator: a heater with metal panels. These get hot and give out heat to warm a room.

reflect: throw back or bounce back.

refrigerant: a liquid that flows around the pipes of a refrigerator. The liquid evaporates easily and takes heat from the refrigerator.

refrigerator: a machine that makes or keeps food cold.

resistance: the attempt to stop something.

rocket engine: an engine that burns fuel to produce hot gas, which drives the engine forward. Spacecraft have rocket engines.

smelting: separating metals from their rocks by heating the rocks so that the metals become liquid and run out.

solar cell: a device which powers a machine by turning sunlight into electricity.

solar panel: a panel on the roof of a building that collects the sun's heat.

solar power station: a building that uses the sun's heat to make large amounts of electricity.

solid: a substance with a definite shape. Most of the objects we use, such as furniture, clothes, and machines, are solids.

steam engine: an engine that is driven by hot steam produced in a boiler. Railroad trains were once powered by steam engines.

storage heater: a heater that contains material that does not let heat pass easily. Instead, the material stores the heat and releases it slowly.

sweat: a watery liquid that comes out of the skin to help cool the body. It also carries away waste.

temperature: how hot or cold something is. Temperature is measured in degrees.

thermometer: a device used to measure temperature.

thermostat: a device that is used to control the temperature of something which produces heat.

tinder: dry material which burns easily. It is used to help start a fire.

tropics: the hottest areas of the world, around the equator.

vacuum: an empty space containing nothing at all, not even air.

valve: a device that opens or closes a hole to control the flow of a liquid or gas.

vapor: a liquid in the form of a gas.

visor: the clear front part of a helmet. The visor protects the eyes.

Index